Transport Through Time

Heather Hammonds

Contents

NELSON
CENGAGE Learning

Australia • Brazil • Japan • Korea • Mexico • Singapore • Spain • United Kingdom • United States

Introduction

Every day, millions of people around the world use different methods of transport.

People travel to school and work in cars, or on buses and trains. Ships and trucks are used to transport goods around the world. Aeroplanes carry passengers and goods long distances very quickly. Outside Earth's **atmosphere**, spacecraft take astronauts and equipment to and from the International Space Station.

Thousands of years ago, people travelled everywhere by foot. Travel was very slow as a person's average walking speed is only four to five kilometres per hour. Today we have methods of transport that can reach speeds of hundreds, or even thousands of kilometres per hour! Travel and transport have changed dramatically throughout history.

Imagine . . .

You are a scientist. You invent a time machine and travel back into the past. You are amazed when you see the world before 2003. Horses and carriages travel the roads, and steam trains stop at railway stations. No aeroplanes have successfully flown yet and space travel is just a distant dream...later on, you travel into the future, too!

Across the Water

Water transport is one of the earliest forms of transport. Canoes and rafts built from wood or rushes have been used for many thousands of years. In some places these types of water craft are still in use today.

More than 5000 years ago, ancient Egyptians built simple boats made of reeds and wood to travel along the **Nile River**. Later, they built large wooden sailing ships. These ships travelled up and down the Nile, carrying goods and people. Egyptians also sailed across the sea, so they could trade with other countries and explore new lands.

A stone carving of an Egyptian boat.

Imagine . . .

You are a crewmember on an ancient Egyptian ship, sailing along the Nile River. Your ship transports grain and animals. You sail past farms and cities on the edges of the river. You see thousands of workers slowly building enormous pyramids!

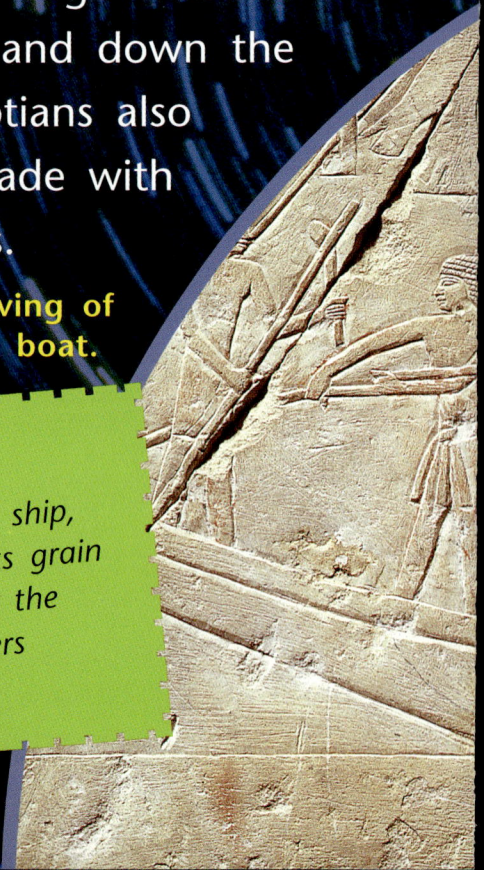

Other ancient peoples built sailing ships, too. The ships were used to travel from country to country, to explore other parts of the world, and to trade goods. They were also used in war.

A Viking ship.

A clipper ship.

Centuries passed and ship design changed. Faster ships with several masts were built. Explorers sailed around the world, exploring different countries. Thousands of people travelled by ship from Europe, and **migrated** to countries such as Australia, the United States, Canada, and New Zealand.

In the mid 1800s, a very fast type of sailing ship, called the clipper ship, was developed. Clipper ships carried goods and people around the world at record speeds.

Different companies competed with each other to sail from country to country in the fastest times.

Clipper ships were some of the last ships with sails to be built. Steam ships powered by steam engines were invented. Steam ships were faster and more reliable than sailing ships.

Today, large modern **diesel-powered** ships are a very important means of transport. Oil tankers carry fuel from country to country. Container ships transport goods around the world, and cruise ships carry passengers on holiday.

Hydrofoils carry people and goods quickly from place to place.

A steam ship.

From Carts to Cars

The most important invention in the history of land transport was the wheel. Before the wheel was invented, people moved goods and heavy objects about on simple sledges or log rollers.

The wheel was invented around 5,500 years ago, in **Mesopotamia**. The wheel was first used to make pottery, but it was soon discovered that the wheel had other uses. Simple, solid wooden wheels were used on carts pulled by animals. These were a much faster means of transport than sledges.

Animals have played an important part in the history of land transport. Animals such as horses, camels and donkeys have been used to pull vehicles or carry goods for thousands of years. In some countries, they are still an important type of transport today.

More than 2,500 years ago, ancient Romans built horse-drawn chariots. Chariots were a fast means of transport, and used in battle. They were also used for the one of the Romans' favourite sports — chariot racing.

Imagine . . .

You are a **charioteer** in ancient Rome. You race your chariot and four horses around the **Circus Maximus**. You must complete seven laps of the track to win. Chariot racing is very dangerous because you go very fast. But if you win, you will become rich and famous.

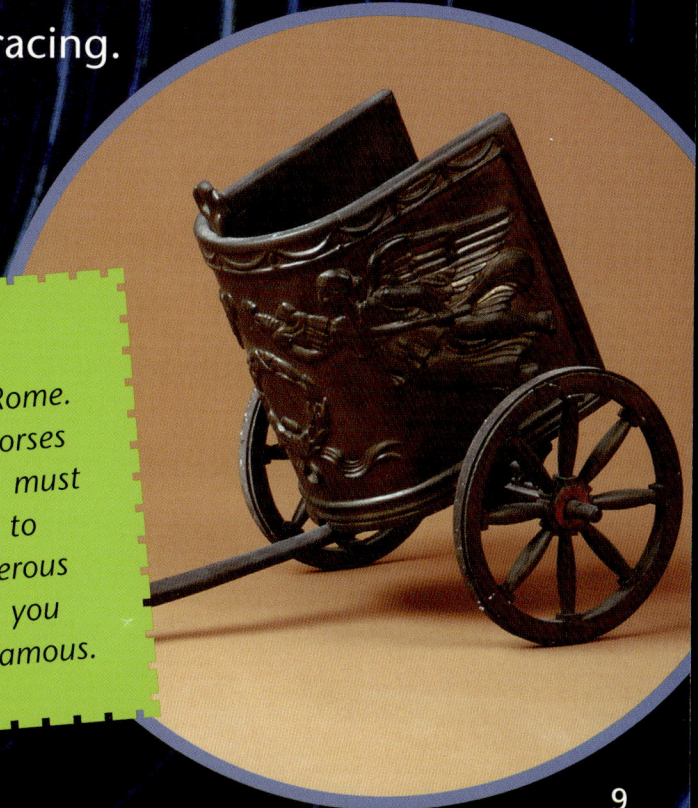

Imagine . . .

You are a stagecoach driver in America's West. You carry passengers, goods and mail. You must travel as fast as possible over bumpy, dusty roads. You stop at different points along your **route** to change your weary horses. You must beware of any outlaws, who try to rob your coach.

As the centuries passed, the design of carts and carriages changed. Heavy carriages, called coaches, were invented. Lighter, stronger wheels were used. Springs underneath the vehicles gave passengers a smoother ride.

By the mid 1700s, fast stagecoaches carried passengers, mail and other goods from place to place. Riding a horse or travelling on a stagecoach were the fastest types of land transport at this time.

The first **self-propelled** road vehicles were built in the late 1700s. They were powered by steam engines.

In the late 1800s, a new type of engine, called the **internal combustion engine**, was invented. Internal combustion engines were smaller and more powerful than steam engines. They ran on petrol or diesel oil, rather than steam.

By the early 1900s, thousands of cars, trucks and buses began to appear on roads around the world. They are the most common form of land transport today.

The Iron Horse

In the early 1800s, the introduction of the steam **locomotive** marked a huge change in transport.

The first useful working locomotive pulled coal at a coal mine in Britain, in 1804.

By the 1830s, passenger and goods **trains** had been developed. Railway tracks for these new machines were laid between cities and towns.

The first working locomotive, 1804.

Imagine . . .

You are a steam train driver on a trans-continental railway. Your job is to watch the controls, stoke the engine and look out for objects blocking the line. The engine is noisy and dirty, and the firebox is hot. But driving a 'modern' steam train is a very exciting job.

For the first time in history, a machine had been invented that could travel faster than a horse. Steam locomotives and trains were often called 'iron horses'.

Steam trains could carry large numbers of people and goods over long distances.

Trans-continental railways were built in places such as Australia, the United States, Canada and Russia. This allowed people to cross entire countries in a few days, rather than trips that lasted weeks or months.

13

Underground railway systems were developed in several large cities around the world. Tunnels were dug deep beneath the city streets and railway tracks were laid. The first underground railway was opened in 1863 in London, England. However, smoke and pollution from the steam trains made travelling underground very uncomfortable.

The first electric railway opened in 1881, in Germany. Electric trains were better suited to underground railways and transport around cities. They eventually replaced steam engines in underground railways.

The first underground railway.

In 1892, the diesel engine was invented. It is an internal combustion engine. The first diesel locomotive was built in 1913. Diesel locomotives ran on **diesel oil** and they were more efficient than steam locomotives. Within 30 years, diesel engines began to replace steam engines. The age of the steam locomotive was over.

Today, electric trains transport people and goods around cities of the world. And diesel trains travel long distances from place to place.

This high-speed French train can travel at speeds of up to 270 kms per hour.

Imagine . . .

You are a locomotive driver, driving one of the longest trains in the world across Australia. You have broken the record for the world's heaviest train. Your train is over seven kilometres long, and is made up of 682 wagons and eight locomotives. It weighs 99, 734 tonnes!

Flying High

People have always dreamed of flying. Leonardo da Vinci, the famous inventor and artist, drew sketches of flying machines more than 500 years ago, but none of these were built.

Leonardo da Vinci's drawings of a flying machine.

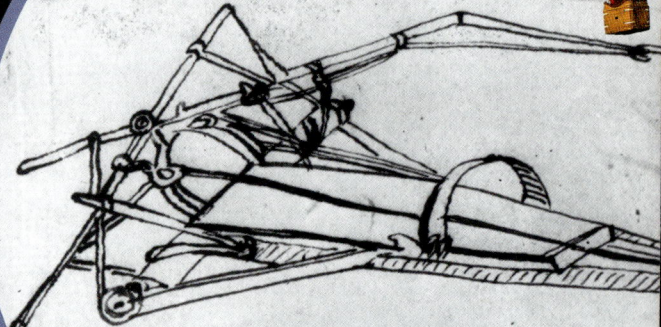

In 1783, two French brothers, Joseph and Etienne Montgolfier, invented the first hot air balloon. They built a hot air balloon from paper and linen. Their first passengers were a rooster, a sheep and a duck.

In that same year, a **hydrogen**-filled balloon was also built and flown. Both types of balloon worked well and balloon flight gradually became very popular.

In 1852, the airship or **dirigible** was invented. Airships were enormous cigar-shaped balloons. Airships were an important form of transport during the early 1900s. They carried large numbers of passengers and cargo long distances.

For many years, airships were filled with hydrogen. Hydrogen is very flammable and several airships caught fire. Today's small airships, or 'blimps', are filled with the safer gas, **helium**.

By 1940, the age of the airship had ended. Faster, more powerful aeroplanes took their place.

Imagine . . .

You are a wealthy passenger on a giant airship, flying from England to the United States. The airship you are travelling on has luxury sleeping quarters, a recreation room and dining room, and it can carry 100 passengers.

GRAF ZEPPELIN

Wilbur and Orville Wright's 'Flyer'.

Aeroplanes have **revolutionised** long-distance transport. Inventors tried to develop engine-powered aircraft throughout the 1800s. At first, they developed successful gliders. Then, engines were added to these.

In 1903, Wilbur and Orville Wright built and successfully flew the first powered aeroplane, the 'Flyer'. The age of the aeroplane had arrived!

Within 20 years of the aeroplane's invention, the first passenger and mail delivery services had begun. No other form of transport was as fast.

Aircraft design was constantly improving. **Jet engines** were introduced to passenger aeroplanes in 1952, making public air transport even faster. Today, huge airbuses and jumbo jets transport people around the world at high speeds.

The **supersonic** Concorde aeroplane is the fastest passenger aircraft today. It carries passengers from New York to London in three hours. Clipper ships took more than 12 days to make the same journey, 120 years earlier.

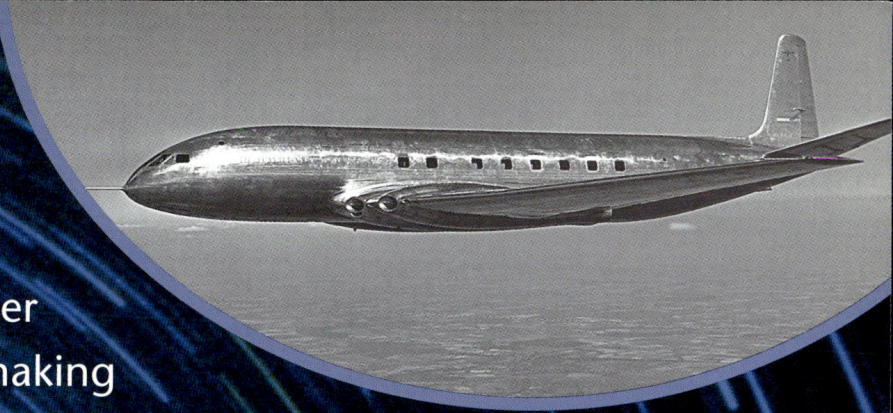

Imagine . . .

You are an aviator, flying some of the first aeroplanes developed. You travel the country, performing daredevil stunts in **barnstorming shows**, and you also compete in air races. One day, you hope to fly solo from New York to Paris, just like Charles Lindbergh. He was the first person to do this, in 1927.

The Space Age

Space travel is the world's newest and fastest type of travel. Space travel became possible with the invention of powerful rockets, during World War Two.

The first object to orbit Earth was the Sputnik satellite, in 1957, and the first manned space flight took place in 1961. In 1969, astronauts from the United States were the first people to land on the Moon. It took four days to reach the Moon, which is around 384,000 kilometres from Earth. This was the longest journey ever made in human history.

In the 1970s,
the first orbiting
space stations were
launched. They were small spacecraft,
with room for only a few astronauts.

Today, the giant International Space
Station (ISS) orbits Earth, 400 kms
above us. Astronauts regularly
travel to and from the station
in spacecraft, delivering new
parts and supplies. The ISS
is due to be completed
in 2005.

Imagine . . .

You are a space tourist, spending ten days on the ISS. You paid millions of dollars for your space holiday. You had to complete a tough training course before you were allowed to travel. A Russian spacecraft transported you to the world's newest travel destination.

A Fantastic Future

Many methods of transport have been developed in the last 300 years. New transportation methods being developed today may be the most popular means of travel in 100 years time.

Most cars, buses and trucks today run on **fossil fuels**, which create pollution. New types of fuel-efficient vehicles have been invented, which are better for our environment.

Fuel-cell vehicles run on electricity. They are powered by methanol.

New types of very fast trains are also being developed. These trains use magnetism to help them to travel at very high speeds.

This train can reach speeds up to 500 kms per hour.

One day, we will travel around the world on sub-orbital liners. Sub-orbital liners will travel very high above Earth, at speeds of over 7000 kilometres per hour.

Space tourism will become more common. Far into the future, people may travel all around our solar system.

The future of transport is looking fantastic!

Glossary

atmosphere the gases which surround a planet

barnstorming shows shows that travelled around the countryside. Aviators performed daring stunts at these shows.

charioteer a person who drives a chariot

Circus Maximus a huge stadium designed for chariot races

diesel oil a type of fossil fuel, made from oil

diesel-powered machines that are powered by a diesel engine. Diesel engines are a type of internal combustion engine.

dirigible another name for an airship — the word dirigible means 'steerable'

fossil fuels fuels formed from the remains of plants and animals that lived millions of years ago

helium a kind of gas that is lighter than air

hydrogen a kind of gas that is lighter than air

internal combustion engine a type of engine that burns fuel inside it. Most engines in cars, buses, trucks and trains today are internal combustion engines.

iron ore a type of rock that contains iron and is used to make metals

jet engines special types of engines generally used on some aircraft that burn fuel and use hot gases to propel them

locomotive a vehicle used to pull or push carriages, trucks or wagons on a railway

Mesopotamia an ancient country in the Middle East that does not exist today

methanol a type of alcohol, made from wood

migrated moved home from one place to another — usually from country to country

Nile River a river in Egypt

revolutionised changed enormously

route a road or path taken to get somewhere

self-propelled something that is able to move itself along and doesn't need to be pulled or pushed by something else.

supersonic something that travels faster than the speed of sound — the speed of sound is about 1220 kilometres per hour

trains groups of railway carriages, trucks or wagons that are self-propelled, or pushed or pulled by a locomotive.

trans-continental crosses a whole continent

Index